D0364000

For Calla and Isla
xx

The Christmas Carrot © 2013 by Allan Plenderleith
For more books by Allan visit www.allanplenderleith.com

First published in this format in 2013
Reprinted in 2014

by

Ravette Publishing Limited
PO Box 876, Horsham, West Sussex RH12 9GH

ISBN: 978-1-84161-375-8

The Christmas Carrot

by Allan Plenderleith

RAVETTE PUBLISHING

Our story begins on Christmas Eve -
an exciting time for one and all.

Unless of course, you're a carrot.

There he is, our little pointy vegetable,
lying on a chopping board next to
an enormous pointy kitchen knife. Gulp!

This time tomorrow he'll be
chopped up and lying in a pool of hot gravy
next to some smelly sprouts.

Or will he?

For THIS Christmas carrot is about
to go where no carrot has gone before.

On an ADVENTURE!

Dad was just about to prepare the Christmas carrot, when his son Billy ran in and grabbed it.

Little Billy took the carrot outside.
The little vegetable could not believe
his eyes. It was snowing!
Big fat flakes fell from the sky.

And there at the bottom
of the garden was a snowman.
But it did not have a nose!
He looked decidedly grumpy.

Billy placed the Christmas carrot right
in the middle of the snowman's face.
It looked very happy!

And a very happy Billy ran back
to the house to have a finger-warming
mug of hot chocolate.

"Aaargh! My nose is running!"
screamed the snowman.

The carrot tried to escape,
but the garden gate was locked!

So he looked for a gap in the fence.

But the snowman was bounding across the garden after him!

Suddenly the carrot saw something
at the bottom of the garden.

A tiny house.

The carrot ran!
The snowman bounced!

But just in time the carrot
jumped into the little house,
safe at last!

"You can't hide from me,
Christmas carrot!"
grumbled the snowman.

The little house was cosy and warm,
with nice soft hay on the floor.

And he was just getting comfy when...

... two glowing pink eyes
appeared in the darkness!

It was Billy's rabbit, Fang!!

"Oooh! You must be my
Christmas present!" drooled Fang,
his sharp white teeth
glinting in the gloom.

It was the snowman!
"That's my Christmas carrot!"
boomed the snowman.

"No, it's MY Christmas carrot!"
screeched the rabbit.

The carrot ran!
The snowman bounced!
The rabbit hopped!

Then the carrot saw something
- a drainpipe!
Quickly, he began to climb!

Finally he made it to the roof –
safe from the rabbit and the snowman.

There he sat for some time,
until the moon was high in the sky.

But suddenly he
heard something... jingle bells!

He turned to see a sleigh, reindeer, and a big man with a red bobble hat jumping down the chimney.

The carrot stepped backwards,
but suddenly slipped,
sliding down the rooftop!

And landed in a soft clump of snow
at the side of the road.

But the others were
on their way after him.

The carrot ran!
The snowman bounced!
The rabbit hopped!
The reindeer flew!

"CATCH THAT CARROT!"

But then the
Christmas carrot
spotted something
shiny in the snow.

A foil tray from
someone's mince pie.

Quickly he jumped inside,
and whizzed down the hill
on his little foil sledge!

Suddenly the carrot hit a bump
and flew through the air!

But he was caught by a red velvet glove.
It was Father Christmas.

Father Christmas
popped the
Christmas carrot
into his
fur-lined pocket.

It was very cosy.

He turned to the others and said "Don't you know that Christmas is about GIVING not GETTING!"

"Sorry Santa..."

And so, safe at last,
the Christmas carrot flew up and away
in Santa's sleigh, over hills and towns
and off through the stars.

When he awoke on Christmas Day,
everything was dark.

Then he heard a voice.
It was Father Christmas.

"Merry Christmas!"

A lid lifted above him
and the carrot saw a face.
It was Mrs Christmas!

"Ooh! A carrot! My favourite!"
slurped Mrs Christmas!

"AAAAAAAAAARGH!"

"CATCH THAT CARROT!"

The end.

Other titles by Allan Plenderleith ...

The Bonkers Banana **(new)**	978-1-84161-387-1	£5.99
The Silly Satsuma	978-1-84161-366-6	£5.99
The Smelly Sprout	978-1-84161-322-2	£5.99
The Boy Giant (paperback)	978-1-84161-352-9	£5.99
The Chicken & the egg	978-1-84161-371-0	£5.99
Princess Chocolate (paperback)	978-1-84161-350-5	£5.99
What Does Santa Do On Boxing Day? (paperback)	978-1-84161-311-6	£5.99

HOW TO ORDER:-

Please send a cheque/postal order in £ sterling, made payable to
'Ravette Publishing' for the cover price of the book/s
and allow the following for post & packing ...

UK & BFPO	70p for the first book & 40p per book thereafter
Europe & Eire	£1.30 for the first book & 70p per book thereafter
Rest of the World	£2.20 for the first book & £1.10 per book thereafter

RAVETTE PUBLISHING LTD
PO Box 876, Horsham, West Sussex RH12 9GH
Tel: 01403 711443   Fax: 01403 711554   Email: info@ravettepub.co.uk
www.ravettepublishing.tel

Prices and availability are subject to change without prior notice.